EVERYTHING IT TAKES

SANDI VAN

An imprint of Enslow Publishing

WEST **44** BOOKS™

Please visit our website, www.west44books.com.
For a free color catalog of all our high-quality books,
call toll free 1-800-398-2504.

Cataloging-in-Publication Data

Names: Van, Sandi.
Title: Everything it takes / Sandi Van.
Description: New York : West 44, 2022.
Identifiers: ISBN 9781978595545 (pbk.) | ISBN 9781978595668
(library bound) | ISBN 9781978595569 (ebook)
Subjects: LCSH: Poetry, American--21st century. | English poetry. |
Young adult poetry, American. | Poetry, Modern--21st century.
Classification: LCC PS586.3 E947 2022 | DDC 811'.60809282--dc23

First Edition

Published in 2022 by
Enslow Publishing LLC
29 East 21st Street
New York, NY 10010

Copyright © 2022 Enslow Publishing LLC

Editor: Caitie McAneney
Designer: Tanya Dellaccio
Interior Layout: Rachel Rising

Photo Credits: pp. 2-19, 22, 27-30, 34-36, 38-41, 43, 44, 46, 47, 49,
51, 54, 56, 57, 59, 60, 62, 63, 65, 67, 69, 70, 72, 74, 76, 78, 80, 83, 85,
87, 88, 90, 92-99, 102-106, 108, 110, 112, 113, 115-118, 120-125,
127, 128, 132, 133, 135-139, 141, 143, 144, 146, 148, 150-156, 158,
160-162, 164-166, 168, 170, 173-176, 178-184 ARENA Creative/
Shutterstock.com.

Printed in the United States of America

CPSIA compliance information: Batch #CS22W44: For further information contact
Enslow Publishing LLC, New York, New York at 1-800-398-2504.

This book is dedicated to my son John, who
appreciates trees nearly as much as I do, and
to all the eco-warriors out there.
Don't give up. The planet needs you.

MY CALLING

The loudspeaker calls us down:

> *All juniors and seniors*
> *report to the cafeteria*
> *for the college fair.*

We follow
like cattle.

Mooing in groups
large and small.

Chewing gum
and checking phones.

Not me.

I'm ready for this.

Questions neatly written
on the last page
of my English notebook.

I'm ready
to leave this town
in my dust.

MY TOWN

feels like a leash
pulled tight.

Whenever
I   try
to   wander.

TOO SMART FOR MY PANTS

Mom tells me
my brain is too big
for my britches.

Which is an
odd way
of saying

I'm too smart
for my pants.

Mom rolled her eyes
at my response,

when I told her:
it's breeches,
not britches.

In the original saying
anyway.

I looked it up.

See?

I'm too smart
for this town.

WORDS MATTER

I'm going to study history
and English.

And then:
    Law School.

Someday,
I will get paid
to argue.

A ROSE BY ANY OTHER NAME

I hate my name.

    Lily.

It means:
    pure
    innocent
    beauty

My parents
must have
thought
I looked
like
a flower.

My older sister says
I looked like
a monkey.

They should have named me

    Vervet.

After the Vervet Monkey.

But they chose Lily.
And I hate it.

NAMES

I wrote about names
for my college essay.

How they shape us.

How they shape what people
expect from us.

I wrote the essay
in poem form.

Because if you want
to get into college

you need to

STAND

OUT.

THE FIRST STEP

The first step
to taking my
dumb
flower
name
and going to
Law School

is getting
into
College.

SO HERE I AM

with the other cattle.

A slow-moving herd
on our way to
the cafeteria.

A group of seniors
in front of me
make bets
on how many pens
they'll collect.

I fear
for
their
futures.

BUT NOT MINE

I'm prepared
with my questions.

I'm prepared
with the list of schools
where I can double major
in history
and English.

Schools
          far
                    far
                              away
                                        from here.

WHAT I'M NOT PREPARED FOR

Every recruiter I talk to
answers my questions.

Fills in the blanks.

Asks a few of their own.

Major?
> Check.

Far away?
> Check.

Required GPA?
> Got it.

SAT scores?
> You know I rocked them.

Great, that's great,
they all say.

*And how about
extracurricular activities?*

...
...
...

JUNIOR YEAR IS SUPPOSED TO BE ABOUT GRADES, NOT CLUBS

I've taken all the right classes.
My grades are good.
Because I spend
my time
studying.
Not trying to
save the world
or make new friends.

Sure, I tried a few clubs—
    debate
    Spanish
    newspaper.
And I'm sure I could
write them down
on the application.

But then,
the recruiters said
there will be an interview.
Where you talk about
your **GOALS**.

And how your time
in **HIGH SCHOOL**
helped you figure out
who you want to **BE**.

ME?

I figured out
who I wanted
to **BE**

by watching episodes
of *Law and Order*
with my mom.

FAMILY

It's just the three of us:
     me
     Mom
     Faith.

When my older sister was born,
Mom had a lot
of faith.

She believed
everything would work out
perfectly—

     husband
     dream job
     beautiful house
     kid
     and then another (me).

The perfect holiday card.

UNTIL

Dad struck it rich
with one of his many
business ventures.

Mom lost her job.

Dad met someone new.

Mom lost in court.

And we had to move
out of the beautiful house
and into this tiny apartment.

How's that for
law and order?

WORDS HAVE DOUBLE MEANINGS

We *need* to *have faith,*
Mom would say.
And I'd look at my sister
and wonder.

Was she planning to leave us,
the way Dad did?

That's the thing
about words.

We need to have
FAITH.

As in:
      Don't give up.

      Follow your dreams.

      Believe they will come true.

And if life
pulls out the rug
from under your feet,
dig your toes
firmly
into
the ground.

LOSS OF FAITH

Eventually
Faith did leave.

But not because
she found a family
she liked better than ours.

(The way Dad did.)

She left to become a dancer
in Las Vegas.

(She had to change her name.)

We saw a video
of her show.

(She looked happy.)

Mom said,
Well, that's life for ya.

Which is
the same thing she said

      when Dad left
      when she lost her job
      when we had
      to leave our house.

(Well, that's life.)

NOT ME

I refuse to allow life
to walk all over me
like an animal
pacing their cage in the zoo.

Life is not something you
let happen.

It is something you grab
with both hands
and steer in the direction
you want to go.

THE NEXT DAY

I watch the
morning announcements
closely
for the first time
ever.

Some girl with a high ponytail
and a guy trying too hard
to grow facial hair
report on meaningless school news.

But then...

*Anyone interested
in saving the planet,*
the girl says,
should come to room B219 after school.

A logo flashes
on the screen.
"Green for Good"
it reads.

I have no interest
in saving the planet.

But I do need a club to join,
and the logo is drawn pretty well.

Okay, I think.
I'll give it a try.
Famous last words.

YOU CAN LEAD A HORSE TO WATER, BUT YOU CAN'T MAKE IT DRINK

I text Mom.
Tell her I'm staying late.

Wander down the B wing
like a lost dog.

No.
A rejected dog.
The one left behind
at the pound.

Because clubs and I
don't exactly stick.

Spanish club:

>   Politely asked
>   not to return.
>
>   I kind of set the
>   Homecoming float
>   on fire.
>
>   They probably
>   shouldn't have
>   put me in charge
>   of the sparklers.

Newspaper Staff:

Question: How hard could it be
to report on the school news?

Answer: When you refuse
to do a piece
ranking soda flavors
in the vending machine–

hard.

Debate Club:

A club about arguing!

A club full of kids
destined for law school!

It should have been
my jam.

But I had trouble
following the rules.

And when I kept
getting disqualified,
they kicked me out.

I picture my college interview:

> *And tell us, Lily,*
> *about your nonacademic*
> *experiences.*

Followed by a blank stare.

I need a win.

I need the environmental club
to work—
no matter what.

So,
I pull my shoulders back.

Smile.

Walk
      through
           the door
                of room 219.

GREEN FOR GOOD

There are five people in the room.

I wonder how they plan
to save the planet
with such limited resources.

> Shush it, Lily.
> No one wants a grumpy
> club reject.

Five faces look up at me
when I enter.

Ten eyes stare at me
like I'm an alien.

> I want to say, I'm not an alien.
> Just a girl who needs to pad
> her college application.

Instead I say,

Hello,
my name is Lily.

I'm here to, um, save the Earth.

It comes off like a question.
I hear someone laugh-snort.

A girl. Dark hair.
Small braids on one side
around her ear.

> *Well you're in the right place,*
> she says.
> *I'm Fiona.*

She raises her eyebrows at the group
and they say their names in turn:

Fern
> *Max*
>> *Cooper*
>>> *Jewel*

> *You new here?* asks Fern,
> a girl with glasses and
> red hair in two long braids.

Yeah, never seen ya around,
adds Max.

Maybe I spend too much time
in the library.

No, I say. *I'm a junior.*

Ah, says Fiona.

She makes the laugh-snort sound again.

A junior, huh?
Here to beef up the ol'
college applications?

Her words are sharp.

I consider walking out.

Finding a different club—
something a bit less
judgy.

But I don't exactly have
other choices.

I need this.

SO... I STAY

Don't look so shocked, College Girl,
Fiona says.

We've seen your type before.

She stares at me.
Her eyes are dark brown,
almost black.

I hold her gaze
as long as I can
and then look down
at the floor.

Let me guess.
Student council dropout?

I shake my head.

No matter.
We're not picky.
We'll take ya.

We need all the manpower—

Person power, Cooper corrects.

Fiona stops.

Grins.

Continues.
Person power we can get.

Here at Green for Good,
we like to get things done.

And extra accomplices
are always welcome.

Fiona winks
at the other group members
who laugh and nod.

I suddenly feel nervous
but also
strangely excited.

So, *College Girl*, Fiona says.

Lily, I say.

Right.

College Girl—
are you in?

ARE YOU IN?

Never have three words
made me feel so excited
and scared half to death.

WANTED: CRAZY GIRL

Their eyes wait.

Am I in for what?
I ask, innocently.
*You planning to blow up
a fracking site?*

Fern giggles.

> *Why? You good with explosives?*
> asks Max.

He grins.

Runs fingers through his
spiky black hair.

Explosives? I—uh—

Don't sweat, College Girl, says Fiona.
He's kidding.

LEADERSHIP

What exactly
are you planning? I ask.

And don't you guys have an advisor
or something?

Cooper points
at a young teacher
in the far corner,
her nose in a book.

       Technically, it's Mix Martin.

Mix? I ask.

We prefer not to assign
outdated gender prefixes.

       Mix Martin is new and
       lets us do our own thing.

       More or less.

Oh.

More
or
less.

FACT VS. FICTION

Look, Fiona says,
we know the rumors
about what we do here.

People say we're
tree-hugging troublemakers,
right?

Did we make a lot of people angry
when we protested the
Memorial Day
balloon launch
last spring?

Yes.

Did we almost get arrested for,
what was it again?

She turns to Fern.

> *Disturbing the peace, Fern says.*

Right, disturbing the peace.

No.

> *The police gave us a warning,*
> Fern says.

And *we're not allowed*
in the party store
anymore.

The party store? I ask.

Cooper explains:

We rented all their
helium tanks.
So the town couldn't.

And we shouted,
BALLOONS KILL WILDLIFE!
during the parade, Max adds.

Fiona smiles,
proud of her team.

And we have never chained ourselves
to trees
to keep them
from getting cut down.

Despite what the school paper
reported last year.

We just stood near them,
says Jewel,
her voice soft and sweet.
And refused to move.

31

She lowers her eyes.
       It didn't work.

But anyway, this is totally tame.
We're planning to pick up trash
near the creek.

Ya know,
the one that runs behind the school?

We're hoping to start a
countywide movement
to clean up the waterways.

MOSTLY LEGAL

Flona motions
to the other
smiling faces
in the room.

We know what people think about us.

But most of the stuff we do
is legal.

Right, gang?

They laugh.

HAVE YOU EVER COMMITTED A CRIME? CHECK YES OR NO

I start to sweat.

Most of the stuff they do
is legal.

Most of it?

NOT ALL TREE HUGGING
AND PROTESTS

I open my mouth to speak,
but Fiona holds out her hand.

I know what you're thinking.
Colleges aren't gonna let you in with
a record.

Stop stressing.

This isn't a protest.
There's no disturbing the peace.
It's just trash.
Trash that doesn't belong
in the water.

Fiona smiles.

Shares a few more stories
about times they
DIDN'T
get arrested.

We get things done.
We find a way.
We play it smart.

And we'll get you in to whatever U
is your top choice.

DINNER: COMPLICATED

Mom is ready
with big helpings
of chicken and rice.

Hungry? she asks.

I nod.

I think about Fern,
who told me she's
named after
the little girl
in *Charlotte's Web*
who rescues
Wilbur the Pig.

And how she doesn't eat animals
because it breaks her heart
to think about their
suffering.

Mom adds salad to our plates,
then tosses the plastic container
into the trash.

How was school?

You find a club to join?

I nod.

I think about Max
who told me he and Jewel
started the school's recycling club.

They loaded
empty soda bottles
and bags of paper
in the back of their
older brother's truck.

Carried them to
a recycling center
every week for months.

Until the school
finally
decided
to help.

Any cute boys in the club?

I shake my head.

I think about Cooper
who prefers the pronoun "they"
and believes
identity and love
should be fluid
and nonbinary.

That's okay, Mom says.

Better to focus on
schoolwork anyway.

THE FUNNY THING?

That's all I've ever done:
      Focus on Schoolwork.

The two hours I've spent so far
with Green for Good
were the strangest

most eye-opening
most confusing
most interesting

two hours
of my life.

MAYBE

it's time for a change.

THE TRUTH

I'd never really given
much thought
to not fitting in.

But the truth
about being someone
who studies all the time,

and then goes home
to watch TV
with her mom:

> There isn't a lot of room
> for a social life.

IT WASN'T ALWAYS THIS WAY

It's not like
I don't have any friends.

Wait.

Okay–

I don't have any friends.

But it wasn't always this way.

Faith and I played
with the neighborhood kids
until we had to move.

And the only person our age
in the new apartment complex

was a kid
who liked to set ants on fire
with a magnifying glass.

Faith and I made our own fun.

Did the best we could
with what we had.

Until she went to high school
and joined cheer.

Found her tribe.

Left me
the way she used to leave
her sandwich crusts.

Alone.

Unwanted.

BUT NOW IT IS

All the things I tried on in
high school
never quite fit.

And my favorite hobbies—

reading books
watching law shows
wandering around the history museum—

are things best done
alone.

ADVICE

I text Faith.

Tell her about the club.

About their
balloon protest.
(She says she'd
heard about it
from her cheer friends.)

About standing
next to trees
but not
hugging them.
(That makes her laugh.)

I tell her
how I want to help
but can't shake
the feeling
that something

is

not

quite

right.

Her advice is simple:

You worry too much,
little sister.

I say, go for it.

GO FOR IT

I text Fiona.
Hey.
This is Lily.

> *oh, hey CG*
> *what's up?*

I type, delete, type.

I had fun today.
Want to meet up
at lunch?

> *liked "I had fun today.*
> *Want to meet up*
> *at lunch?"*

I'll take that as a yes.

LUNCH: COMPLICATED

Girls like me,
you know
the ones who don't have
(m)any friends.

We don't hide in bathroom stalls
and eat lunch on our laps
as movies may lead
you to believe.

Girls like me,
who don't enjoy
the constant chatter
of cafeteria convos.

We seek out
a quiet place
and sweet-talk
our way in.

For me,
the quiet place
is the back corner
of the library.

In an old study carrel
once used
for in-school
suspension.

Faded drawings
and curse words
carved into
every inch.

I like to run my fingers along the words,
so often misspelled,
and wonder what became of the kids
who wrote them.

I agreed to help
restock the bookshelves
in exchange
for my secret hideaway.

Key word: SECRET.

I don't want
Fiona to know
that's where
I eat lunch.

So today,
I carry my brown bag,
suddenly aware of its
environmental wrongness.

I carry my brown bag
into the upper-class
cafeteria
and search
for my new

(dare I say it?)

FRIENDS.

HOW THE OTHER HALF LIVES

The cafeteria is noisy.
Too noisy.

Sounds bounce off walls
in an uneven rhythm.

I find Fiona and her friends
in the back corner.

At least we have that
in common.

College Girl! Join us!

The table smiles and
makes space.

I look around at everyone.
Smile back.

Where's Jewel? I ask.

Little Sis? says Max,
as if he's trying
to remember
where he left her.

Freshman Cafeteria.

He points
across the hall.

Fiona pats the empty chair.
Sit. Eat.

I sit.

But I don't eat.

Too nervous to share my meal
with an audience.

STRANGEST ENTRANCE EXAM EVER

I *meant to ask you
the other day,* Fern says.
Why did you pick us?

I think about lying
but decide
the truth is easier.

> *I want to be a lawyer.*
>
> *And to get into
> a good college,
> you need
> extracurricular activities.*
>
> > *So, Fiona was right,*
> > Max says.

It's more of a statement
than a question.

I nod.

*But why did you
pick us?*
Fern asks again.

Why Green for Good?

I don't want to admit
my failures at
every other club.

Don't want to get
kicked out
of this one
on my second day.

I shrug.

> *Never really thought about it.*
> *Your logo was cool—*

>> *That's Jewel, Max*
>> says proudly.
>> *She's the artist.*

A *lawyer, huh?* Fiona asks.
Following in
the family footsteps?

My face feels warm.

> No, *my dad,*
> he—*he invests in*
> *local businesses.*

(Mom's words. It always
seemed to me like he threw
money at crazy ideas.)

*He owns that
new health food
chain—
Life Fuel.
And my mom,
she works for the town.*

Fiona raises her eyebrows.

Really?

I nod.

*Always good
to have connections
in government.*

Fiona offers me
a slice of
apple.

I guess that means
I passed their test.

*Well, then,
welcome to the team.*

A WALK IN THE WOODS

After school,
we exit the building.

Wheel our buckets behind us.

Two each:
    one for trash
    one for recyclables.

Gloves for everyone.

Fern explains the
importance
of staying safe.

Don't pick up
broken glass
or needles.

And if you see anything
strange,
call for the others.

If we see anything
strange?

I must look confused.

Because she adds,
We've heard stories.
Sometimes people do
shady things
under the cover
of trees.

The day is warm and windy.

I pull my jacket tight
and slip on my gloves.

Wander through the woods
behind our school.

Head toward the creek.

Bend down to pick up trash
along the way.

walk
stop
walk
stop

LITTER ART

I pick up old coffee cups
with chewed-up rims,
piles of beer bottles
and cigarette butts,
gum wrappers,
damp scraps of loose-leaf paper:
     an old math test
     biology notes
     a list of Spanish verbs.

Life discarded
by people too lazy
to find a trash can.

AWAKENING

We wander deeper,
deeper into a part of the
woods I've never
wandered through before.

We wander
in different directions.

Voices fade.

The only sounds:

>   the crisp crunch
>   of fallen leaves
>   beneath my feet
>
>   the quiet flow
>   of the creek
>   traveling over rocks.

As I walk into the trees
and away from everything else,

>   away from school,
>
>   away from the group,
>
>   AWAY—

my chest feels looser,
my legs stronger.
Something cracks open
inside me.

I stop.

What is this feeling?

THE CALM BEFORE THE STORM

I stop.

Soak in the feeling.

I stop.

Hear my name.

THE DISCOVERY

LILY!

My name echoes
through the trees
like a birdsong.

Is someone hurt?

OVER HERE! I answer.

COME QUICK!

WE FOUND SOMETHING!

SOMETHING BIG!

I follow the shouts.

Wind my way
through the woods
until I find the rest
of Green for Good.

They say nothing.

Fern points to a spot
covered by thick grass.

Everyone's eyes follow.

I stare.

What am I looking at? I whisper.

As if the woods could hear me
talking about it.

Telling its secrets.

Fiona's feet follow
Fern's outstretched finger.

*This, my friends, Fiona says,
is more than our
little group can handle.*

*This, my friends,
is a problem.
A huge problem.*

IF IT'S A HUGE PROBLEM

then why is Fiona smiling?

SCENE OF THE CRIME

Fiona motions us closer.

We examine the scene.

The way investigators do
on crime shows.

Rusty hunks of metal
and old car batteries lie
half buried in the dirt.

Fiona pushes
the metal aside
carefully
with her boot.

Digs further into the dirt.

Finds a plastic tarp.

Pulls.

Look, she says.

There are several barrels
with chunks rusted out.

The water around them
shines and shimmers
in the afternoon sun.
Like a greasy pan
left in the sink.

Cooper bends down,
scoops some of the water
into a small container
like the ones we use
in science lab.

Jewel snaps pictures
on her phone.

Fern lifts rocks
and makes strange whistling sounds.

Fiona keeps smiling.

*This is what
we've been
waiting for*, she says.

WAITING

Fiona looks around at each of us.
Stops at me longer
than everyone else.

Or maybe that's my imagination.

Is she afraid
to admit something
in front of the new girl?

We've been trying
to make a statement
for what,
three years now?

About the pollution
in our community.

And does anyone listen?

No.

Does anyone care?

No.

They don't.

People don't worry
about pollution.

They don't worry
about protecting the planet.

But now our town will have to listen.

They'll have to care.

Dumping waste like this into the creek?
Which flows all the way through town?

She looks at Cooper,
who swirls dirty water
inside the container.

This is big.

This is Town Hall Big.

TOWN HALL BIG

Fiona's smile spreads
across her face.

College Girl,
didn't you say something
about your mom
working for the town?

When's the next
board meeting?

I swallow.

Fiona waits for her answer.

Second Thursday of the month, I say.

That's the night
Mom comes home late
with takeout from the Indian Buffet
across the street from the town hall.

Perfect, Fiona says.

Soon, but with enough time to prepare.

Cooper, get the water tested.
Fern, search for changes in
the local wildlife.

College Girl,
swing by my house
Saturday
to talk more.

She takes her gloves off
and types something into
her phone.

My phone pings.

No turning back now.

ALL'S WELL THAT ENDS WELL...

But this is just the beginning.

We load our bags
into Max's truck.

*We'll talk more at
next week's meeting, Fiona says.*

Great work, everyone.

Great work.

WHAT NEXT?

That night,
I consider telling Mom
what we found.

Consider asking her
for help.

My mouth opens,
but the words
don't come out.

I'm too afraid
she'll say no.

That she'll say
some things are better
left alone.

But.

There are probably
kids who play
near that creek.

I think about
the rusty metal,
the shimmering water.

Wonder what sort of
chemicals
are leaking
from the barrels.

Wonder what it's been doing
to the fish and birds.

It's not safe.

Fiona is right.

We need to take a stand.

I pull out my phone.
Stare at her address.

We need to do what's right.

THE HOUSE WHERE FIONA LIVES

is small and white,

tucked at
the end of a lane
like a secret.

Purple wildflowers
line a path
that curves toward
the front porch.

Two rocking chairs sit–
waiting.

A woman with long, black-gray hair
and Fiona's near-black eyes
greets me at the door
with a smile and nod.

Tips her head to the right.

I follow it.

See Fiona at
the side of the house,
kneeling,
hands in the dirt.

College Girl!
Come help me plant these bulbs.

She pats the ground next to her.

I look down at my clothes—
gray sweater over black leggings.

Not exactly garden wear.

DIGGING IN THE DIRT

Fiona sits back on her heels.
Laughs a bit too loud.

C'mon,
the dirt won't hurt ya.
I promise.

She pulls on my hands.

I nearly fall into her lap.
Face caught up in her hair.

It smells like the tea
Mom makes when
my stomach gets upset.

Sweet.
Spicy.
Strangely calming.

Fiona helps me to my knees.
Passes me a shovel.

It's easy.
Dig.
Place.
Cover.

She digs a hole.
Places the bulb at the bottom.
Covers it with dirt.

Dig.
Place.
Cover.

You try.

I am much,
much slower.

But I follow her motions—
filling the earth
with pale white bulbs.

Their flaky skin falls around us.
My fingernails fill with dirt.
I lose myself in the repetition.

When we finish,
I am covered in sweat
and dirt
and happiness.

GREEN THUMB

Thanks for the help, College Girl,
Fiona says.

*You aren't half bad at the whole
gardening thing.*

> *Thanks. I used to help my mom
> at our house—
> before we moved, I say.*

> *She said I had a green thumb,
> and I thought she meant
> there was something wrong with it.*

I laugh.

So does Fiona.

Her loud belly laugh.

> *We're in an apartment now.*

> *Not much space for
> stuff like this.*

*I bet you could
find some,* she says.

Not asking why I had to move.

Not nosing her way into my wounds.

Rooftop garden, maybe?

I nod.

    Maybe.

GRAMS

Fiona heads toward the house.

Well, now that I've used you
for the free labor,
guess we can go inside
and get some drinks?

Talk about what we'll say
at the meeting?

I nod again.
Follow her onto the porch.

The woman from before sits
on one of the rocking chairs.

That's my grams,

Fiona says.

She touches the woman
gently
on the knee.

Uses her hands to sign something.

Motions toward me.

Lily, Grams.

I realize she's introducing us.
Hold out my hand,
but she doesn't take it.

She tips her chin
slowly
toward her chest
and smiles.

I turn my outstretched hand
and wave instead.

She lifts her chin.
Gives a small wave back.

She got sick as a kid, Fiona says,
and lost most of her hearing.

She's super sweet
but doesn't trust people
until she gets to know them.

But don't worry, College Girl,
you're all right.

She'll like you.

HAWK

The inside of Fiona's house
looks cramped and lived in.

With mismatched chairs
around the kitchen table.

Four on each side
and two on the ends.

Cartoon noises spill out
of the room down the hall.

You have a bunch of
brothers and sisters? I ask.

She nods her head.
   And cousins.

   Grams helps take care of all of us
   in one way or another.
   After school, on the weekends,
   longer when our parents are away.

I don't ask her
what her situation is.

   We'll go up to my room.
   It's quieter there.

Posters cover the walls
of her bedroom.
Famous people speaking out
against animal abuse.

Waterfalls.
Fields of flowers.
A hand-drawn bird,
Jewel's name in the corner.

>*That's me, as a hawk.*
>*Cool, yeah?*

Plants line her windowsill.
The room smells like sweet earth.

>*Tell me your tips--*
>*for getting the town*
>*to listen,*
>she says.

But I don't hear her.
Not really.

I can't stop staring at
the hawk.

That's amazing, I say.

Point at the drawing
in case she isn't sure
what I mean.

>*Oh, Jewel's pic?*
>*Yeah, that girl's got talent.*

Too bad she can't seem
to get out of
Max's shadow.

She draws people in their
true form.
Or so she told me when she did it.

Fiona.
The Hawk.

Grams smiled when she saw it.

In our culture,
the hawk means:
        strength
        courage
        vision.

I can only hope, right?

I think you have a lot of courage
to take this on, I say.

Thanks, Lily.

She uses my real name.
The one I hate.

But when she says it,
it sounds smooth and full of silk.

It makes my heart race.
It sends sparks into my fingertips.

DOWN TO BUSINESS

I tell Fiona what I've learned
at other town board meetings.

How you have to:
      be prepared
      be polite
      speak clearly.

You wouldn't believe
some of the things
people complain about,
I say.

That mess near the creek—
it's serious.

I think we can

get the town to help.

Really.

      Good, Fiona says.

      Guess our lawyer chose to
      walk into our club meeting
      at the perfect time.

Me?

Fiona nods.
>I'll do the talking, of course,
>but you write the argument.

>That's what lawyers do,
>right?

Right.

DON'T JUDGE A BOOK BY ITS COVER

The next week,
our English assignment
is to write a short story
with an idiom
as the moral.

An idiom
is a common saying—
like *it's raining cats and dogs*
or *don't cry over spilled milk.*

Weird sayings
are my thing.

It's clear
the universe is
on my side
today.

But then—
the teacher explains
she will assign each of us
our idiom.

What happened to:

Free Will
and
Freedom of Choice?

My idiom:
Don't bite off more than you can chew.

I stick the pencil tip
into my teeth.

Attempt to chew through
the plastic.

Obviously
not what the idiom means.

I raise my hand.

This is meant to be fiction, yes?
I ask.

Because it's starting to feel
more like real life.

HOW?

Is there a right way
to write what we want to say?
Words, chosen with care.

How do we convince the board
to make someone have to pay?

MERRY-GO-ROUND

Town board meetings are
like watching
the merry-go-round
go around
and around
and around.

Metal animals
bob up and down
in circles.

The same music
plays on repeat.

Town board meetings are
my mom calling roll
over and over
as each board member
agrees to a line item
they already agreed to
earlier that day.

Town board meetings are
like that annoying commercial
that plays every time you
stream music.

Mom says court rooms are
like that, too.

She says TV makes them
look like fun,
action-packed
thrillers.

But the reality is:
slow motion,
repeat.

The reality is:
careful line item
review.

The reality is:
don't miss
any details.

Or else.

I say,
I'll watch
the same metal horses
ride up and down,
listen to the same commercial
over and over,
if it means I can
save someone from
losing everything.

EVERYTHING IT TAKES

That's the thing, you see.

Dad left.

Dad found a family
he liked better
and replaced us
like a pair of
broken sunglasses.

Mom should have
walked away
with everything.

But Dad had
a better lawyer
who knew how to
play the system.

Mom should have
walked away
with everything.

But that lawyer
stripped us
down
to nothing.

Not me.

I promised Mom
that I would
fight
for the underdog.

Fight
for what is right.

I promised Mom I'd do
everything it takes.

WHO?

It occurs to me
just now
that
sometimes
the underdog
isn't a person.

Sometimes it's
our planet,

burning
flooding
breaking.

Who fights for it?

SOMETIMES

Sometimes,

you prepare for a big thing:
        a project
        a test
        a performance,
        a town board meeting.

And you give it
all you've got.

But
you
come
up
short.

WHAT HAPPENS

The board thanks us
for our efforts
with the creek cleanup.

Says:

> *How wonderful to see*
> *young people*
> *making a difference.*

But they won't help
clean up the waste
right now.

They say it probably
didn't really make a dent
in the ecosystem.

It's not "top priority."

THERE'S GARBAGE IN THE WATER

The truth of it is:
There's garbage in the water,
and nobody cares.

GREEN FOR GOOD

doesn't give up.

We find a way,
Fiona said
at my first meeting.

I believe her.

But in the back of my mind
sits the other thing she said
that first day:

Most of what we do is legal.

Which means
some of it
is not.

CATCH-22

I'm invested now.

I want to see
the trash cleaned up.

I want to see
someone punished
for polluting the water.

But I've worked
too hard and
too long
to give up
on my own
dreams.

LEARNING TO FLY

Fiona's Grams
is my new favorite person.

I visit every day.
Plan our next steps.

I'm learning
how to sign.

Can say:

> *hello*
> *thank you*
> *beautiful*

When she sees me,
she holds
her fingers
and thumb
together
and drags them
across her nose.

Fiona says that's
the sign for flower
because my name is Lily.

It means Grams likes me.

IT'S ALWAYS LOUD AT FIONA'S HOUSE

Fiona and I sit
on the front porch.

Sounds spill
from the open windows.

                    talking
            laughter
                    television
                            music
            video games

Grams sits on her chair,
quietly rocking
back and forth.

Her eyes flutter
open and closed.

Ya know, I get it from her,
Fiona says.

What?

The activist bug.

When Grams was younger,
she served as a water protector.

Kept some big corporation
from dumping chemicals
into the creek on our land.

I'm talking: laid her body down
and refused to move
until the government
stepped in
and did something.

That's what we need to do,
College Girl.

None of this "wait for the
paper pushers to decide stuff."

We need to lay our bodies down.
We need to take action.
We need to do—

I finish her sentence
because I know
what she will say.

She feels the same way
about the Earth
as I do about the law.

She watched her family
get pushed around.

Not in the same way
as mine, obviously—

but when you feel
stepped on
mistreated
taken advantage of,

the shoe may be different,
but the pressure on your spine
the pressure on your heart
can feel the same.

We need to do
everything it takes,
I say.

WHERE DO WE GO FROM HERE?

Fiona grins.

One of those grins
that start small
and grow bigger
until they cover
a person's face.

I could kiss you right now, she says.

And I'm not sure if she's serious
or if that's what she says
to all the people
who fall for her
charm.

BUT SHE DOESN'T KISS ME

Not yet.

INSTEAD

We go online.

Research toxic waste.

Study the town map:
        landfills
        waterways
        possible culprits.

Figure out what
to do next.

As Fiona explains,
when you have a weed
in your garden,
you can't snip the top
and not expect it to
grow back.

You need to grab it out
at the root.

We need to cover all
our bases.

We *need to grab it out
at the root.*

METAPHOR

I'm good at understanding
metaphors.

But what exactly
is the root
in this scenario?

PLATE, CUP, EVERYTHING RUNNING OVER

Fiona adds to my plate
already overflowing with

schoolwork
housework
college apps.

Deadlines lurk
around the corner.

Choices nag at my brain:
early decision
or early action,
where
and
when.
Weighing the risks–
possible rejections
application costs.

Can we even afford it?

Mom suggests I apply to the
local community college.

Just to start, she says.

Does that mean
there isn't money
for anything else?

Financial aid,
scholarships—

I wish I had
someone to talk to
besides the counselor at school
who always forgets my name.

I feel lost—
unimportant.

What makes me think
I can do
any of this?

What makes me think
a college would want
ordinary
nose-to-the-grindstone
me?

THE ROOT

Fiona texts me
with her latest plan.
To search for nearby
businesses who may
have been dumping
waste into the creek.

She's narrowed it down
to a few possible places.
Followed a path from
the creek out to Main Street.

*Someone had access
to those woods,
she says.*

*Someone knew they
could hide their waste
where no one
would see it.*

> *How do we figure out
> who it was?
> I ask, innocently.*

A little
too innocently.

Because I know
what her answer
will be before
she says it.

The town hall
keeps records
of that very thing,
going back
for years.

ESCAPE

Mom and I sit on the couch,
brains fried,
hands lost in
bowls of salted popcorn.

Scrolling through
the streaming menu
for a new law show to binge.

You okay, Lil? Mom asks.

A trailer starts on the screen
while she looks at me,
eyes full of concern.

Sure, yeah, just stressed.

Well, you know what they say, right?
Stressed is desserts spelled backward.

I don't know why,
but her strange wordplay
makes me laugh out loud.

Makes me laugh and laugh
until I fall off the couch.

Mom says, *It wasn't that funny.*
But she laughs, too.

We laugh and laugh
until tears form
on the edges of our eyes.

Times like this
I remember how
she's my best friend.

THE CHOICES WE MAKE

When we stop
and catch our breath,
Mom says,
Lil, it'll all work out.

Take one thing at a time.

She smiles.

Holds my chin in her hand.

Like she used to do
when I was little.

And I think:
could I freeze this moment
with Mom protecting me
forever?

Telling me
it will all work out.

And I think,
Will it?

If I help Fiona sneak
into town hall,

I'll betray the one person
who has always stood by my side.

A NEW FRIEND

But the moment that
thought flashes
through my mind—
something else flashes.

My phone.

Go ahead, Mom says,
her hand back at her side.

    It's probably Fiona, I say.

My words a quick mumble.

You talk about her a lot, Mom says.
It's nice to see you found a new friend.

She emphasizes the last word
and I can't tell if it's because she
thinks there's something more
between us.

Or maybe,
maybe,
Mom doesn't trust
Fiona.

I pick up the phone.

Open the text.

It's from Fiona
to everyone in the group.

No greeting.

Just a green light—
it's go time.

I look down
at my pajama pants
and slippers.

I should stay here
with Mom.
Comfortable.
Safe.

I'm about to respond
when another text comes in—
also from Fiona
but addressed only to me.

Don't let me down, CG,
followed by a kissing winky face.

WHAT DOES IT MEAN?

What does it mean
when the girl you like—
the girl who terrifies and excites you—
sends you a kissing winky face?

It means:
      You put on
            a pair of pants
                and sneakers
                    and
                        GO.

YOU CAN'T MAKE AN OMELET WITHOUT BREAKING SOME EGGS

I tell Mom that Fiona
needs notes for the calc exam
even though we aren't in class together.

I don't make eye contact.

Terrified she'll know
what's truly in my heart.

Can I borrow the car? I ask.
I'll be quick, I promise.

Sure, Mom says.

Her voice full of
disappointment
but layered
with hope.

She only wants the best for me.
This I know.

But who's to say what
the best truly means?

DESTINATION: DECEPTION

In the car,
I stare at Fiona's text.

Stare at the kissing winky face.

Think about it
way more than I should.

Feel my heart race
for more than one reason.

Set out
for our meet-up
destination

and wonder
if anything will ever
be the same.

ARRIVAL

The
parking
lot
is
lit
by
a
single
streetlight.

It flickers:
> bright
> dark
> bright
> dark

My car sounds
like the rumble
of an arriving plane.

Fiona walks toward it,
backlit.

Fern and Cooper
appear behind her,
their bike brakes
screeching.

Max and Jewel
exit from his truck.

They all stand
like a group of bandits
ready to break
into a bank.

PRICE OF ADMISSION

They all stare
at me.

Alone.

On the outside.

Will they ever accept me?
Is this what it will take?

And what
exactly
is
THIS?

This is not
how you get
into law school.

SEALED WITH A KISS

College Girl, Fiona says.

She wears a grin across her face.

Like a kid who discovered
her mom's secret stash
of candy bars.

Welcome.

Glad you could make it.

Her words are oddly formal,
and I feel trapped by them.

She walks over to me
     and under
          the single
               streetlight–

in front of everyone–

kisses my cheek.

REWRITE

After this,
I'm going to have to
rewrite
my college essay.

New title:

*How I Got Arrested for Breaking into
Town Hall*

by Lily Landon

THE TRUTH IS:

We're not breaking in.
Because I'm here,
and Fiona knows
I have a key.

Fiona knows
I have a key
because she asked me
to bring it.

She asked me
to bring it,
and I slipped my hand
into my mom's purse.

I slipped my hand
into my mom's purse
and stole her key.

SOMETHING YOU NEED TO KNOW ABOUT ME

I've never done anything like that before.

GOODY TWO-SHOES

That's what Faith
used to call me
because I was the one
who followed

all
the
rules.

I was the one
who pointed out
the legal
ins and outs
of every situation.

Faith would roll her eyes
and pinch the spot
between my neck and shoulder
until I squealed,
and Mom yelled at us
to stop messing around.

The only time I ever lied to Mom
was a *lie of omission*—
which means
it wasn't technically a lie.

Because I never
SAID
anything.

The night Faith
snuck out
to the dance studio
to record an audition tape.
     (Mom told her it was a
     waste of time and money,
     but Faith saved her pennies
     anyway.)

Faith made me SWEAR
I wouldn't say anything to Mom.

That night,
I felt the sweat
seep through my T-shirt
and prayed
Mom wouldn't ask me
anything
about Faith.

Mom bought her story
hook, line, and sinker,
as they say.
She never asked me what I knew.

So, I never had to actually
LIE.

Until now.
Tonight.

I guess this is what
teenagers are
supposed to do?

GANG OF THIEVES

Fiona puts her arm around me.
Pulls me close,
like suddenly we're a couple.

We walk like that
toward the door.

And I want to feel excited
because I like Fiona.

But I can't help but wonder
if she's using me.

Thanks for doing this, Fiona whispers
in my ear.

> *No problem,* I say,
> even though I don't mean it.

It could be
a *big* problem.

TIME IS MONEY

We enter the building
easily.

My hand shaking
as I slip the key
into the lock.

It's an old building.

Small town.

No cameras.

The street behind us
is quiet.

Mom's office is this way, I say,
pointing down the dimly lit
hallway.

*But do you have a plan
for exactly what you need?*

My voice cracks.

There's a beat
while I wait for someone
to break the silence.

Finally, Max says,
	*We need to find out
	who's responsible.*

*Maybe this is a bad idea.
Maybe we should just file an
official complaint?*

(That's what the board
suggested we do.)

I try to pretend like
I've forgotten our loss
at the meeting.

Forgotten how they told us
they'd look into it,
the way a parent says *we'll see*
when you ask to go
to the amusement park.

You know it will never happen.
But you hold on to hope
anyway.

I wait for an answer.

Wait, as five pairs of eyes
stare at me.

My gut says
RUN!
RUN!
while my heart thuds,
and my feet freeze in place.

Finally, Fiona speaks.

We did file a complaint.
We spoke at the meeting.
We followed the rules.

No one listened.

Now it's time to take action.

There have to be
records stating ownership
and land sales for all
the businesses in the
plaza that backs up
to the woods.
That waste is relatively
fresh, so we need records
from the last
three years.
We need to connect the dots
about who would have
access to hazardous waste.

I swallow.

There are records—I know it.

I know there are
because I helped Mom
organize her office
last summer.

    We looked online, Cooper says,

but so many shops
changed hands in the
past couple years
and the town's website
is crazy-outdated.

Please, Lily, will you help us with this?

I hesitate.

Think about what's on the line.

Fiona looks at me
with eyes I can't seem to resist.

Someone needs
to protect the woods, she says.

Our woods.

Someone needs to—

> *Please don't say*
> *"speak for the trees,"*
> Max says.

She doesn't have to.

SOMEONE

Fiona closes her eyes.

Opens them.

Grams always says, someone needs
to stand up for the land
because the land
is what helps us stand.

So, I ask you, College Girl,
the same question I asked when
you first walked through our door.

Are you in?

THE RECORDS

I lead the group down the hall
and use Mom's keys to
open up the office.

Know exactly where to go
because I've spent
plenty of afternoons
doing homework
at the round conference table.

Watching, waiting maybe,
for a moment such as this.

We search for the records,
careful to keep things
in their place.
My hands sweat
with guilt.

I *think this is it*, Fern says,
a folder in her palm
dated last year.
There's a map inside
with businesses labeled
and numbered.

She sets it on the table,
and we all examine it
like a patient
with strange symptoms.

There it is, Fiona says.
Points.

*That's where we found
the barrels.*

She traces with her finger
back toward the road.

Private landowners.
Commercial shops.

One name sticks out.

*An auto shop, yes!
Those car batteries.
I bet this is it,* Fiona says.

I look,
see the name,
and nearly pass out.

Landon Automotive.

THE HISTORY OF DECEIT

You see,
before Life Fuel,
(The health food store
that helps you do more!)

Dad invested in
a dog-grooming business
(even though we
never owned a dog).

And before that,
a vacuum cleaner supply store.

He tried his hand
in all sorts of
different business ventures.
Some had success
and some failed.

BACK TO THE BEGINNING

But *before* all of his success,
Dad worked in an auto shop
to help pay for his
business school courses.

And then he bought the shop.

Put his name on it.

Kept the building for years.

Last spring,
he sold the building
for a pretty price.

But first, he
likely had to
clean house.

Leave without
a trace–

his specialty.

Rusted oil barrels.
Old car batteries.
The trash
was his.

WHITE AS A SHEET

Fiona puts her hand on mine.

Hey, College Girl, why does it look
like you're about to pass out?

Do I tell them the truth?

I already feel entwined in
this mess,
like a poisonous vine
choking a tree.

THE QUESTION IS:

Am I the tree?

Or am I the vine?

CAN'T HIDE FROM THE TRUTH

It's Cooper
who figures it out.

Landon Automotive.
Isn't that your
last name, Lily?

I think about lying.

Really think about it.

Think about keeping
my mouth shut
for once.

   Yeah, I say, *it's my dad's.*

    Did you know
    he was doing this? Max asks.

Keep it shut,
Lily.
No one needs to
hear your drama.

    He doesn't exactly
    talk to us
    anymore.
    So, no.

SHAME

Eyes look away.

Ashamed for me.

Of me.

No one speaks.

Until Fiona steps
in front of
the map,
folds it back up.

Look.

*It's not about blame.
It's about solutions.*

*It's about making a difference
and getting things done.*

BROKEN

Fiona pulls her shoulders back
the way TV lawyers do
before their big
closing argument.

I know everyone wants
to protect the woods.

The truth is,
we don't have the resources
to fix this on our own

To safely remove the trash
and clean up the water.

We need help.

Everyone nods,
although Fern looks like
she's about to cry.

> I played in those woods
> as a kid, Fern says,
> her voice barely above
> a whisper.
> Used to catch frogs
> in the creek.
> But when I went looking
> last week, I couldn't
> find any.

Jewel rubs Fern's back.

Fiona's right.
We need help.
We need to find a way
to fix this.

Lily, does your dad still live
in the area?

Now I'm the one who looks like
she's about to cry.

FORGOTTEN

I nod.

A quiet
acknowledgement
of defeat.

He lives here,
in this same
small
stupid
town,

and never
ever
comes
to see
me.

RUN

The truth—
that awareness
of what really,
truly
is—
hits me like a
tree branch
in a windstorm.

Sudden.

Hard.

Knocking me off
my feet.

Sending
me out of
the room
down the hall
into the
parking lot,
breath fast
and sharp
in my gut.

I don't turn around
to see if anyone
followed me.

I don't want to be followed.
I don't want to be pitied.
I don't want to be forgotten.

But I was.

We all were.

Me
Mom
Faith

Dad left without warning.

And took a piece
of each of us
with him.

NOT ALONE

The light
in the parking lot
flickers
like something out of
a horror movie.

Fiona comes out
alone,
hair blowing gracefully
in the wind.

For a moment,
I'm distracted by
how calm
and beautiful
she is.

You okay, Lily?
My name, like sweet sugar
to a hungry bee.

I nod.

Sure, now my brain has
decided to be silent.

My dad left, too,
she says softly.
When I was a baby.

Mom struggled
to pay the bills.

So she decided
to enlist.

She's been deployed
twice.

That's why we live
with Grams.

But even when Mom's home,
it's like she's not.

Like her mind is always
someplace else.

I'd wondered where her parents
were, but knew better
than to ask.

Having to face the truth
about your family
when your family
is broken,
makes *you* feel
broken.

ONE

You know why I care so much
about my health and the Earth?
Fiona asks.

Because we only get one.

One body.

One mind.

One planet.

Everything I learned as a kid
about how my family fought
to protect the land,
to respect it,
brought me
to moments like this.

I refuse to pollute my body.

I refuse to pollute my mind.

I refuse to pollute the Earth
or let anyone else destroy
the place I call home.

Fiona walks over.

Holds my hands
in hers.
I like you a lot, Lily,
and we should probably have
a conversation about that kiss
from earlier.

She grins,
and I feel my face
light on fire.

But right now?

We need to find a way
to clean up the woods.

And make your dad pay
for what he did.

All of it.

THE PRICE OF BETRAYAL

We walk back inside.

Put everything back
the way it was.

Guilt eats at me
from the inside out.

I've betrayed Mom
the way Dad did.

But I tell myself
it's for a good cause.

All of this
is for a good cause.

RISING ABOVE

I used to think
this was all about me.

Getting into college.
Getting ahead.

I used to think
this was all about
rising above.

Now I wonder
if rising above
means
stepping on
everyone
below
you.

POLLUTED

After all–
half of Dad's
DNA
flows through me.

Flows through me
like a dirty river.

Polluted.

SECRETS

Fiona doesn't tell the group
about our conversation
in the parking lot.

And I get the feeling
they don't know
her full truth either.

We agree to meet the next day
after school
to discuss the plan.

And when we leave,
she squeezes my hand
in hers.

FIRST

We file an official complaint.

Not against the town,
but against my dad's
old company.

The building stands empty.

The auto shop closed before
Dad sold it last year.

He never explained why
he sold it.

Only that it was time to
move on to bigger,
better things.
He wiped the slate clean
and started over.

The way he did
when he left us.

And now he's going
to pay.

YOU CAN'T KEEP RUNNING FROM YOUR GHOSTS

Fiona told me
she spent a long time
being angry at her folks.

Angry at her dad for leaving.
Angry at her mom for not
being able to deal.

But then
she realized
there were people
who *did*
stand by her.

Her siblings,
her cousins,
aunts and uncles,
Grams.

People who hadn't let her down.

THAT MORNING

I give Mom a big hug.

What's this for? she asks.

You need something from me?

Could she see the guilt
on my face?

I keep it buried in her shoulder.

Words muffle against
the soft fleece of her shirt.

>   *Nah, just want you to know
>   I love you.*

She pulls away.
Looks in my eyes
to check for
drugs
lies
guilt.

I smile.

Aw, sweetie, I love you, too, she says.

And I'm proud of everything
you're doing
with your club.
It's changed you
somehow.
Opened you up.

I want to tell her
about what we found.

Want to tell her
about Dad.

But I don't want to
open old wounds,
and I know she'll
ask me how I know.

So, I keep that
piece of
the puzzle
hidden

for now.

NEXT

We put together
what Fern calls
a "CTA":
Call to Action.

Jewel records a video
of the trash
and plays it on the
morning announcements.

High-ponytail girl tells
the school:

We need to ACT NOW

in the perky way
that only she could
pull off.

Max gets permission
to go from class to class
with a petition
we can use
to support our case.

Cooper leads
a cleanup crew
after school
out past the athletic fields
into the woods
with bags, barrels,
and gloves
to get started.

It all happens so quickly
that I feel inspired
to do what I had been afraid
to do.

To do what Fiona said
I had to do.

It'll be good practice,
she says,
for when you're a big-shot
lawyer.

BIG-SHOT LAWYER

I used to think
that the first step to
reaching my goal
was to get into college.

But the first step
was really
finding something
to make me
want to
fight.

THE POWER OF WORDS

Fiona helps me draft
the argument.

Helps me choose
the perfect words.

She loves words
almost as much as
I do.

       Now what? I ask
       after we finish the letter.

Now, the real fun begins.

THE LAST STEP

I haven't spoken to my dad
since Faith graduated
from high school
and left for
Las Vegas.

He stood
at the edge of
the crowd.
Waited
to congratulate
his daughter
and wish her well.

Mom smiled
her Mom-smile,
and said something
about how it was nice
that he came.
I wondered
if he would come
to my graduation, too.

Congratulate me
and wish me well.

Now you don't have to
wait for graduation, Fiona says
when I tell her the story.

I have to face the music,
push past the ill will,
and ask for his help.

PRACTICE MAKES PERFECT

Do you ever do the thing
where you practice a
conversation in your head
before you see someone?

Practice, practice, practice,
each word
carefully chosen–
like picking out the
perfect prom dress.
But then you see the person
and your tongue clogs your
mouth like hair in a drain.

Your brain forgets
all the things
you'd practiced.

And after, you
walk away
wondering
what just happened?

You realize the moment
you tried so hard to make right
crashed and burned.

It won't be like that,
Fiona promises.
You have the speech.

THE SPEECH

I will win people over with words.
I will win people over with words.
I will win people over with words.

REALITY

Here's what I think will happen:

Fiona will (somehow)
get in touch with my dad
and ask him to meet with us
to talk about
how he needs to
take responsibility
for the mess.

I will be brave
and strong
and full of
confidence.

Tell him it is
time
he did the
right thing.

He will try to
make excuses,
but then apologize
and vow to make
it better.

(In the true fantasy,
he'll vow to make
it ALL better.)

That's not what happens.

Because my dad
refuses to talk to Fiona.

And so she tells me
she'll do
everything it takes
to get
his attention.

BLINDSIDED

Fiona tells me to meet her
in the school's back parking lot
at 3 p.m.

I do.

Dad isn't there.

In his place,
a news crew.

Cameras.
Microphones.

A woman I recognize
from the five o'clock news.
Fiona,
wearing a bright green T-shirt.

She sees me,
smiles,
passes me a shirt.

We had them made,
she says,
ignoring the look
on my face.

The one that says,
what have you done?
I put the T-shirt on:
GREEN FOR GOOD
in bold letters
across my chest.

The newscaster
approaches us.

Explains how we should
look at her
and not the camera
when we speak.

I nod my head.
Still in shock.

She adjusts my shirt.
Says, *Ready?*

I nod again.
This is it.

FIVE O'CLOCK NEWS

I'm here at Hamilton High School
with Fiona Silversmith
and Lily Landon,
two students from the
environmental club,
Green for Good.

During a routine campus
cleanup, they found something
they'd never expected.

Stay tuned to learn more.

I wait for the break,
but we keep filming.

The newscaster interviews
Fiona first,
asks her about the club—
how it started,
what we do.

Fiona talks about
the importance
of keeping our
waterways clean
and how chemical waste
needs to be properly
disposed of.
She is a natural.

Then, it's my turn.
I clear my throat.
Take a deep breath.

Explain how we traced
the trash back
to an old auto shop
(not giving away
our secret break-in)
and how we're asking
the guilty party
to come forward and help
with the cleanup.

I ignore the newscaster's
instructions.

Stare right into the camera.

> The shop
> on Main and West Ave
> was called Landon Automotive,
> and we're asking the former owner
> to step up
> and take responsibility.

My words are clear.
I wonder if people will make
the connection to my last name.

I wonder if Dad will watch
the news and see his daughter
calling him out.

The camera focuses away from us
and back on the newscaster.

There you have it, folks.

Two young activists
doing what they can
to keep our town
clean and safe.

ACTIVIST

A word I never thought I'd use
to describe myself.

A word that meant someone
who causes scenes
who makes noise.

A word I now know
means someone
who dares to make
a difference.

LATER THAT SAME DAY

I rush home
to tell Mom
the news

before she sees
me *on*
the news.

Her face is a mix
of proud and scared.

She's always done
everything in her power
to protect me.

And now
I've gone and exposed
the truth
of our family.

The ugly truth.

THE UGLY TRUTH

How did you find out?
Mom wants to know.

I have no choice
but to confess.

I tell her about
the stolen key.

Pray she forgives me.

She's silent for
a million breaths.

You put my job at risk,
she says,
so quietly
I barely hear.

This is how I lose
my best friend.

I know
I'm sorry
can't fix it,

but I say it anyway.

CONFRONTATION

At 5:15 the phone rings.

Dad.

Mom puts him on speaker.

He yells for a minute
about airing dirty laundry
and did she have anything
to do with his
public humiliation?

Mom raises her eyebrows at me
but says nothing.

I picture Dad's face in my mind.

Picture him with his eyebrows
pointed down
in anger.

I think about my words
and choose them carefully.

Hi, Dad. It's Lily.
You know,
your daughter?

I'm sorry if you feel
embarrassed right now.
But I'm not sorry for what
I did.

And I hope you make the right choice
for our community.

I hope you do
what needs to be done.

I hope you fix
everything you broke.

Yeah, okay,
I realize
I'm not just talking
about
the
creek.

CLICK

Mom presses the screen
to hang up
before Dad has a chance
to respond.

Tilts her head at me
and shakes it
ever so slightly.

We have some things
to discuss
but I want you to know
that I will always
have your back,
Lily.

I will never leave you.

We'll get through everything
together.

MOM CONTINUES

But right now
it appears there's
someone here
to see you.

I look out the front window
at someone looking up
and trying to figure out
which apartment is ours.

Fiona.

THE DATE

Hey, College Girl,
she says when I meet her
on the front steps.

Nice work today.

   Thanks, you too.

I tell her about the phone call
with my dad.

She laughs when I describe
his imagined eyebrows.

Then she does something
I've been hoping for.

*So, you wanna go grab a coffee
to celebrate? There's a new vegan
bakery I've been wanting to check out.*

   Are you asking me out on a date?

Fiona smiles and flicks her hair
behind her shoulder.
I'll take that as a yes.

MY FIRST DATE

Over coffee and pastry,
I tell her the good news.
How I've decided to apply for
environmental studies
with a concentration in law.

> *You've really inspired me to*
> *make change in the world,* I say.

Aw, you're just sucking up
because you want me to write
a recommendation.

I laugh.

Speaking of which, Fiona says.
She pulls out a letter.

It's from Grams. She wanted to tell you
that she appreciates what you did.
Not sure if you can use it for college, but–

I hold the letter against my chest
and feel the positive energy
flow through it.

COURAGE AND CONFIDENCE

Oh, and one more thing.
This is from Jewel really, but I
kinda asked her to draw it, so—

Fiona holds out another piece of paper.
It looks like the one she has
in her room
of her, as a hawk.

Only this one is me,
as a bear.

Fiona explains:

Bears represent courage
and confidence.

They fight for what's right.

They stand up for the truth.

Just like you, College Girl.

MAKING WAVES

That night,
instead of our
usual law show,
Mom and I watch
the late-night news.

They replay our story.

Mom tells me I'm grounded
(for stealing the key
and breaking her trust),
but she gives me a hug.

I'm impressed, baby girl.
You're well on your way
to making waves.

FIGHTING FOR THE UNDERDOG

After the part with Fiona and me,
the newscaster talks about
a new movement to
clean up local waterways.

Explains how people can help.

The story closes
with a shot of Fern
standing near the creek
holding a frog.

Do it for the frogs, she says,
as it jumps from her hand
and lands in the water
with a tiny splash.

WANT TO KEEP READING?

If you liked this book, check out another book
from West 44 Books:

Our Broken Earth
By Demitria Lunetta

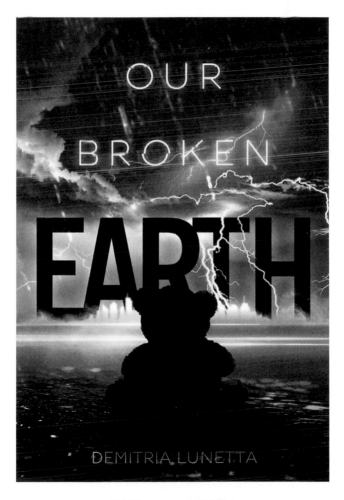

ISBN: 9781978595408

1

The earth hates us.

With its rising tides
              and poison winds
                          and angry sun
                                     and toxic rain.

It's raining now.

None of us dare to brave the storm.

Not for anything.

2

"Mal!"

Kurtis screams.
   He's two years younger than me.
   Fourteen, but small for his age.

"The rain! It's getting in!"

There's a leak and the unpleasant stuff drips down.

Kurt panics, but
I grab a metal bucket.
   Rusted.
   Worn out.
   Broken.

Like everything here.

3

We huddle inside the

one room that we call ours.

One room in an apartment with ten.

One room in a building with hundreds.

One room in a block with thousands.

Jaynee tells me that

one family used to live in each apartment in
this industrious, expensive, seaside city.

It feels like a lie. It is too much space for one family.

But...

4

Jaynee knows
        things.

Jaynee knows
        that there used to be more land.

Jaynee knows
        that it was not always this hot.

Jaynee knows
        the water that falls from the sky wasn't
        always bad.

To walk in.
To bathe in.
To drink without it
        burning your throat and
        turning your insides to mush.

5

I watch the rain

   drip

into the bucket.

And
   with each drop, the foul water splashes a little
   onto the rim.

And
   soon it will eat through the worn wooden floor.

And
   we will fall through to the family beneath.

And
   we will have nowhere to go.

CHECK OUT MORE BOOKS AT:
www.west44books.com

ABOUT THE AUTHOR

Sandi Van is a writer, counselor, and self-proclaimed tree hugger from Buffalo, New York. She is the author of young adult verse novels *Second in Command* and *Listen Up*, and her poetry won recognition in the *Elmira Star-Gazette* and the PennWriters' In Other Words contest. She hopes her story will inspire readers to do their part to keep our planet beautiful and safe for everyone.